MS WIZ BAN

Terence Blacker has been a full-time writer since 1983. In addition to the best-selling *Ms Wiz* stories, he has written a number of books for children, including the *Hotshots* series, *The Great Denture Adventure*, *The Transfer*, *The Angel Factory* and *Homebird*.

What the reviewers have said about Ms Wiz:

"Every time I pick up a Ms Wiz, I'm totally spellbound . . . a wonderfully funny and exciting read." *Books for Keeps*

"Hilarious and hysterical." Susan Hill, *Sunday Times*

"Terence Blacker has created a splendid character in the magical Ms Wiz. Enormous fun." *The Scotsman*

"Sparkling zany humour . . . brilliantly funny." *Children's Books of the Year*

Titles in the Ms Wiz series

All *Ms Wiz* titles can be ordered at your local bookshop or are available by post from Book Service by Post (tel: 01624 675137).

Terence Blacker

MS WIZ
BANNED!

Illustrated by Tony Ross

MACMILLAN
CHILDREN'S BOOKS

First published 1990 by Piccadilly Press Ltd

Young Piper edition published 1991 by Pan Macmillan Children's Books

This edition published 1997 by Macmillan Children's Books
This edition produced 2001 for The Book People Ltd,
Hall Wood Avenue, Haydock, St Helens WA11 9UL

ISBN 0 330 34870 1

7 9 8

A CIP catalogue record for this book is available from
the British Library.

Phototypeset by Intype London Ltd
Printed by Mackays of Chatham plc, Chatham, Kent

CHAPTER ONE

A Friend In Need Is A Friend Indeed

Just because you can do a few magic spells, and fly, and turn people into animals now and then, it doesn't make life any easier. Sometimes being a Paranormal Operative can be really hard work.

"Yes," said Ms Wiz, putting the telephone on to boil. "Being magical is no bowl of cherries, that's for sure."

She was in her flat and had a tough day ahead of her, doing her homework, learning new spells and revising the old ones.

Then there was the housework. Ms Wiz looked at the list of things to do which she had pasted on a notice-board in her kitchen. It read:

1. Tell the vacuum cleaner to do the bedroom.
2. Put a washing and ironing spell on a dirty pile of clothes.
3. Speak roughly to the duster about the book shelves which haven't been touched for weeks.

"Flats don't clean themselves, you know," she said to Herbert, the magic rat, who was asleep in the corner.

"You can help me by cleaning out your cage right now."

Herbert twitched his nose and went back to sleep.

"Just a quick cup of tea," Ms Wiz said to herself. "Then I'll get on with those spells." She glanced at the telephone and sighed. It was true what people said – a watched telephone never boils. Just then the teapot rang.

"Hullo," said Ms Wiz, picking up the lid.

"Er, you won't remember me," said a man's voice from the teapot. "But I'm a school inspector. We met once at St Barnabas School."

Ms Wiz smiled. The last time she had seen the School Inspector, he had been running across the playground without his trousers on after Herbert the rat had run up his left leg.

"Of course I remember you," she said.

"We have a bit of a crisis here," said the School Inspector. "I wouldn't have called you but you're my last hope. We need your help."

"Tell me about the crisis," said Ms Wiz.

"Well," said the School Inspector, "it all began at yesterday's morning assembly . . ."

*

4

It had all begun at yesterday's morning assembly.

The highlight of assembly at St Barnabas was when the Head Teacher Mr Gilbert spoke about his Thought for the Day. This lasted for five (or, if it was a particularly big Thought, for ten) minutes and could be about any important subject.

One day the Thought might be "A Friend in Need is a Friend Indeed." Or "Great Oaks from Little Acorns Grow." Or "Neighbours, Everybody Needs Good Neighbours."

The children of Class Three liked Mr Gilbert's Thought for the Day. It gave Katrina the chance to finish the homework she should have done the previous evening. Her friend Podge used those few minutes to eat a couple of chocolate biscuits he had brought in his pocket. And Podge's friend Jack, who always went to bed too late, could catch up on some sleep.

But yesterday, the day of the crisis, Mr Gilbert's Thought had been most unusual.

"I think," he said, "I think I'm going to be sick."

Because so many of the children were busy doing their homework, or eating, or sleeping, no one paid much attention. But then Mr Gilbert sat down heavily on one of several empty chairs in the front row.

At that moment, Miss Peters leapt to her feet and said quickly, "Now, children, until Mr Gilbert feels better, we'll sing our favourite song, 'Lord of the Dance'." She sat down at the piano and, with a brave smile, began to sing "Dance, dance, wherever you may be."

"He won't be doing much dancing," whispered Katrina to

Podge, as the Head Teacher tottered down the aisle and out of the door. "Who's going to run the school now? Miss Gomaz, Mrs Hicks and Mr Williams are all ill too."

"Perhaps we'll all be sent home," said Podge when he had finished his biscuit.

". . . Otherwise they'll all have to be sent home," the School Inspector said to Ms Wiz the next day. "We need someone to run the school for a week. We're desperate."

"You want me to be the head of St Barnabas?" Ms Wiz could hardly believe her ears.

"And we need other teachers too," said the School Inspector.

"Leave it to me," said Ms Wiz. "Your crisis is over."

"And, er, Ms Wiz." The School

Inspector sounded embarrassed. "May I make one small request?"

"Of course."

"Go easy on the magic, all right?"

Ms Wiz sighed. Why *was* it that people were so nervous about a few spells these days?

"Trust me," she said.

At the next morning's assembly, the children of St Barnabas noticed that there was a stranger sitting in the Head Teacher's chair. She wore a dark suit, a black gown and had a funny square hat on her head.

"She doesn't look much fun," Caroline whispered to Katrina.

"Come back Mr Gilbert, all is forgiven," said Katrina.

The woman stood up and said quietly, "Good morning, children. My name is Miss Wyzbrovicz. I'm

Mr Gilbert's replacement. I'd like to introduce you to my two assistants who are here to help me this week."

From the front row, a small, neat woman in glasses and an older, grey-haired man stepped forward and stood on each side of her.

The new Head Teacher took off her hat, and shook her head, allowing long dark hair to fall on her shoulders. Then she started clicking her fingers. "One, two, three, four," she said.

To the astonishment of everyone in assembly, the woman's two assistants started clapping their hands in time.

"What on earth?" muttered Jack who, for the first time in living memory, was awake during assembly.

Suddenly the Head Teacher began to talk – or rather to sing.

"Morning, everybody, get into that beat,
Listen to me, children, and tap those
    feet."

"I don't believe it," said Katrina.

"The Head Teacher's doing a song," said Podge.

"It's morning assembly and your feet's a-tappin'
As you hear your new Head Teacher a-rappin'."

Now the grey-haired man joined in, singing,

"My name's Mr Warlock, now listen to me,

I'm here to teach ya some geographee."

"A rap song?" said Jack, his jaw sagging. "At St Barnabas morning assembly?"

The other teacher stepped forward.

"I'm Miss N Chanter but don't be
afraid
I'll show you how magic potions are
made."

"Magic potions!" Caroline smiled. "That must be it. When things get this strange, there can only be one person behind it."

"Of course," said Podge. "Look at the black nail varnish on the Head Teacher's hands."

Soon the whole of Class Three were clapping in time to the song.

The Head Teacher smiled, pointed the fingers of both hands at the children and sang,

"So, kids, I'm here to teach you the biz
You know me, my name's—"

"Ms Wiz!" shouted everyone in Class Three.

Outside the School Hall, the School Inspector listened. He had a busy day ahead, but was just calling by to see that the new Head Teacher was settling in all right. From the sounds coming from assembly, she seemed to be getting on well, even if it was a bit noisy.

"Phew," he said, glancing at his watch. "At least there's no magic around."

CHAPTER TWO

Travel Broadens The Mind

No magic?

The children of Class Three who clustered around Ms Wiz after assembly were shocked by the news she brought them.

"What about Herbert the rat?" asked Caroline.

"And flying around the classroom on your vacuum cleaner?" asked Katrina.

"And turning teachers into warthogs?" asked Jack.

Ms Wiz held up her hands for silence.

"The School Inspector has invited me to St Barnabas on condition that there's no magic," she said.

The children groaned.

"Why?" asked Katrina.

"Because spells make grown-ups nervous, that's why," said Ms Wiz, putting on her square hat. "So I'm going to be a serious Head Teacher."

"Who's in charge of Class Three this week?" asked Caroline. "Mr Williams is off sick."

"I've given you Mr Warlock," said Ms Wiz. "I think you'll find him very interesting, but this is his first teaching job. Can I depend on you to be nice to him?"

"You can depend on us," said Jack. "We're Class Three."

"That's what worries me," said Ms Wiz.

"Is it true that you're a wizard, sir?"

"Jack!" hissed Caroline. "Remember what Ms Wiz said."

Mr Warlock stood at the door of the

classroom and stared in amazement at Class Three.

"Excuse me for asking," Jack continued, ignoring Caroline. "It's just that I've got a book at home called *Witches, Warlocks and Other Weird Creatures*."

Katrina put up her hand. "And the other new teacher's called Miss N Chanter," she said.

"Nicola Chanter, yes," said Mr Warlock.

"N Chanter. That means that she *enchants*, doesn't it?"

Mr Warlock took off his glasses, laid them on the desk and looked at Class Three very seriously.

"I don't know what you're talking about," he said. "I'm just as normal as any other teacher."

"Which isn't very normal," murmured Jack.

"All right," said the new teacher. "Answer your names, please." He read

out the register. There was only one person missing and that was Carl, the youngest boy in the class.

"Carl's always late," said Lizzie. "He probably thinks it's a Saturday."

The teacher frowned and made a note of Carl's name.

"Now today we're going to do some geography," he said, unrolling a map of the world that he had brought with him and pinning it on to the blackboard. "Who likes geography?"

There was silence from Class Three.

"Learning map signs," muttered Podge. "Discovering the difference between an isthmus and a peninsula. That's really interesting, isn't it?"

Mr Warlock looked surprised.

"Well," he said, reaching into his briefcase, "I think you'll like it after today."

He laid a box on his desk and took out three darts.

"Who knows the capital city of Norway?" he asked.

Caroline put up her hand.

"Oslo," she said.

Mr Warlock gave her a dart.

"And the highest mountain in the world?"

Jack put up his hand.

"Mount Everest," he said.

Mr Warlock gave him a dart.

"And who can give me the name of a major European city where there are no pedestrian crossings?"

There was silence. Mr Warlock smiled and put up his hand.

"Venice," he said. "Because all the streets are canals." He gave himself a dart. "Well done, Mr Warlock," he said.

"This is a *normal* teacher?" muttered Jack under his breath.

"Now, the two children with darts should come to the front of the class and throw them at the map," said Mr Warlock.

Caroline went to the front and threw her dart. Then Jack did the same. The teacher was about to throw his dart when Katrina asked, "What's this got to do with geography, sir?"

Mr Warlock looked surprised.

"Didn't I tell you?" he said. "I'm

taking you on a field trip to the most interesting place one of the darts lands on."

Caroline looked at where her dart had stuck in the map.

"Mine's in Milton Keynes," she said. "And Jack's is in the middle of the Atlantic Ocean."

"Oh dear, that's not very interesting," said Mr Warlock. He threw his dart, which made an odd humming noise as it flew through the air.

"Where did it land, Caroline?" he asked.

Caroline looked closely at the map.

"On a small island called Sombrero," she said. "It's in the Caribbean Ocean."

Mr Warlock smiled. "That's more like it," he said.

"I still don't see what's wrong with

Milton Keynes," muttered Podge, but no one was listening.

It wasn't that Carl meant to be late for everything. It was just that things were always happening to him that didn't happen to other people.

On this particular morning, for example, a cat followed him down the street. Since he was going towards a main road, he had to take the cat back to where he had first seen it. But then the cat followed him again. He took it back. On his third trip, carrying the cat back, its owner came out of the house and thought Carl was trying to steal it. It took quite a long time to explain the problem, by which time Carl was late for school yet again.

Nervously, he knocked on the Head Teacher's door.

"Come in," said a voice from inside.

Carl was surprised to find a woman sitting at Mr Gilbert's desk. She was playing chess with a rat.

"I was looking for Mr Gilbert," he said.

The woman smiled. "I'm Head Teacher this week," she said. "You can call me Ms Wiz."

"Ms Wiz!" said Carl, who had only

come to St Barnabas that term. "I've heard about you. You're the person who appears whenever a bit of magic's needed, aren't you?"

"That's right," said Ms Wiz. "Now what's the problem?"

Carl took some time to explain why he was late for school.

"I went to my classroom but no one seems to be there," he said.

"Really?" Ms Wiz looked concerned.

"All I could find was a notice on the blackboard," Carl said. "It read, 'GONE ON A FIELD TRIP TO THE SUNNY TROPICAL ISLAND OF SOMBRERO – BACK SOON!' What could that mean?"

"I think," said Ms Wiz, who had gone quite pale, "that it means I'm in dead trouble."

CHAPTER THREE
Ask No Questions,
Hear No Lies

"I *knew* it," said Ms Wiz, as she
hurried across the playground with
Carl running behind her. "I knew
those two would start casting spells
as soon as my back was turned."

"Which two?" Carl asked.

"Mr Warlock and Miss N Chanter,"
said Ms Wiz. "They're both
Paranormal Operatives. Magic is as
natural to them as flying."

As *flying*? Carl frowned. "But why
didn't you just tell them to be
normal?" he asked. "After all, you are
Head Teacher. They're supposed to
be able to boss people around."

Ms Wiz groaned. "I'm just not the
bossing kind, I suppose," she
muttered.

When they arrived at Class Three's empty room, Ms Wiz went straight to the map on the blackboard and pulled out three darts that were sticking into it.

"Oh no," she said. "Warlock's been using his magic darts again – and he's left them behind. Heaven knows how he'll get Class Three back here again."

Carl was looking at Class Three's lockers. "They won't be here for lunch anyway," he said. "They've taken their lunchboxes."

Ms Wiz sighed. "We'd better go and see Class Four," she said. "I don't trust Miss Chanter either."

As they entered the classroom next door, Carl couldn't help noticing that there was an unusual number of pet rabbits hopping about the room.

"Wow," he said. "I never knew Class Four kept rabbits."

Miss Chanter smiled and looked around the room.

"The class don't keep rabbits," she explained. "They *are* rabbits. If they can't spell properly, I'm turning them into—"

"No no *no!*" shouted Ms Wiz suddenly. "No magic, no spells, no rabbits, no potions, no broomsticks! I've already lost Class Three to a sunny tropical island. Turn these rabbits back into children immediately."

Grumbling, Miss N Chanter uttered a spell. Before Carl's astonished eyes, the rabbits became children once more.

"That's better," said Ms Wiz. "From now on, Miss Chanter, it's the three R's for Class Four. Reading, writing and—"

"Rabbiting about?" suggested Jamie, a small red-haired boy sitting at the back of the class.

"No," said Ms Wiz. "Responsibility. I expect you all to be responsible while I try to get your friends in Class Three back from the other side of the world."

"Well, really," said Miss N Chanter, after Ms Wiz and Carl had left the room. "She used to be such fun before she was Head Teacher."

"It's always the same," said Jamie. "Class Three get the excitement and we get the telling off."

"Yeah." The rest of the class joined in. "It's really unfair, Miss."

The teacher scratched her head thoughtfully. "Perhaps I could take you on a trip around town," she said.

"We've seen the town," said Mary, who was sitting beside Jamie. "We live here."

"Yes," said Miss N Chanter. "But have you seen it from the sky?"

*

Ms Wiz had the nastiest surprise imaginable when she returned to the office with Carl. The School Inspector was waiting for her.

"Good morning to you, Ms Wiz," he smiled. "I was just passing by and I thought I'd look in to see how you were getting on."

"Er, quite well, thank you," said Ms Wiz nervously. "Everything's going swimmingly."

"And who's our young friend here?" the School Inspector asked, nodding in Carl's direction.

"He's in Class Three with Mr Warlock," said Ms Wiz.

"They've gone on a field trip," said Carl quickly.

The School Inspector nodded. "Where to?" he asked.

Ms Wiz had turned quite pale. Then she straightened her back and said, "I cannot tell a lie. Mr Warlock appears to have taken them to Sombrero."

"And where precisely is Sombrero?"

There was another silence, during which the clock in Mr Gilbert's office could be heard ticking.

"It's a small island in the Caribbean," said Ms Wiz weakly.

It was at this moment that Carl saw something out of the office window which attracted his attention. Miss N Chanter was opening a door and a flock of pigeons was following her into the sunlight. One of them was the same colour red as Jamie's hair.

"Are you telling me that an entire class has disappeared to the other side of the world?" There was a faint hint of panic in the School Inspector's voice. "Am I to understand that there has been magic on these premises in spite of my specific instructions?"

Ms Wiz nodded miserably.

The School Inspector leapt to his feet.

"Right, that's it," he cried. "Rats up trouser legs are one thing – disappearing children are quite another. I'm calling the police and then I'm going to the Town Hall. I'll get you banned for life! Now, please pack your things and go. You will not be allowed back on the premises."

"But, sir," said Carl. "How are you going to get Class Three back if you ban Ms Wiz?"

The School Inspector looked at Carl as if he were about to swat him like a fly.

"There are such things as aeroplanes," he said nastily.

After he had left, Ms Wiz slumped into her chair.

"I should never have agreed to be a Head Teacher," she groaned. "Magic and a sense of responsibility don't seem to go together."

"Oh well," said Carl, anxious to cheer her up. "At least he didn't see the pigeons."

"Pigeons? Did you say pigeons?"

"They just walked out of Class Four's door and flew off," said Carl.

Ms Wiz had buried her face in her hands and was making an odd moaning sound.

"Let's just hope they're homing pigeons," said Carl.

The sun shone brightly on the lovely tropical island of Sombrero. The waves of the bright blue Caribbean lapped softly on the white sand and a gentle breeze carried the sound of calypso guitar across the beach. It was certainly the best field trip that Class Three had ever been on.

Katrina and Caroline sat under a palm tree, listening to a man playing a guitar, fanning themselves with their exercise books. Jack had found a skateboard ramp nearby and was showing the local children some tricks. Podge had cracked open a coconut and was using the top of his pen as a spoon. Lizzie was collecting seashells, and the rest of the class were paddling in the waves.

"Anyone got the time?" asked Mr

Warlock, sleepily sipping an orange drink through a straw. "We must remember to get back home before tea-time."

"Haven't you even got a watch?" said Lizzie, as she inspected a starfish.

"Must have left it at home in my case," said Mr Warlock. "It's probably with the magic darts."

"So how are we going to get home then?" asked Lizzie.

"That's just what I was wondering," yawned Mr Warlock sleepily. "I expect Ms Wiz knows the spell."

CHAPTER FOUR

Look Before You Leap

One of Mr Gilbert's favourite Thoughts for the Day was "When One Door Closes, Another One Opens." If Ms Wiz had been asked for her Thought this particular day, it might have been "When One Door Closes, The Ceiling Falls Down On Your Head." Or . . . "Just When You Think Things Can't Get Worse, They Do." Or . . . "Help, Get Me Out Of Here!"

Class Three had disappeared to the other side of the world.

Class Four had taken wing and were flying around in the clouds.

The School Inspector was reporting her to the police and was about to get her banned from the school.

"The important thing is not to panic," said Carl, as they sat in the Head Teacher's study, wondering what to do next.

"Yes, good, absolutely right," said Ms Wiz, panicking.

"If we can just get the two classes back by the end of the day," said Carl, "we can pretend that the School Inspector invented it all."

Ms Wiz sat up straight in her chair and looked at him sternly.

"I cannot tell a lie," she said.

"Of course not," said Carl. "Anyway, you're magic. I'm sure you can do it."

Ms Wiz sighed. "But I don't know the travelling spell," she said.

"Oh dear," said Carl gloomily.

"Of course, Miss N Chanter knows it but she's too busy being a pigeon to be much use."

"Oh dear, oh dear," said Carl even more gloomily.

Ms Wiz stood up suddenly, picked up her chair and walked towards the door.

"We'll just have to go and get help," she said. "Bring your chair to the playground, will you, Carl?"

"My *chair*?" Bewildered, Carl followed her out of the room, carrying his chair.

Moments later, amid a loud humming noise, Carl and Ms Wiz were hovering a few feet above the playground.

"Flying chairs!" Carl gasped. "Don't we need seat belts?"

"Of course not," smiled Ms Wiz. "This is magic."

The chairs rose high above the school, turned slowly towards the east and rose into the clouds.

"Where are we going?" Carl shouted above the sound of the wind whistling past his ears.

"Headquarters," said Ms Wiz.

Headquarters? Carl remembered Lizzie saying that she had seen Ms Wiz's home, an old car, when she had helped rescue Lizzie's cat from burglars, but no one had ever mentioned headquarters.

"Is it far?" he asked.

"Beyond Ongar," said Ms Wiz.

Beyond Ongar! Carl had never heard of Ongar, let alone a place beyond it.

Soon the chairs were descending rapidly through the clouds, coming to rest in a quiet back street in front of a tall office block with dark windows. By the entrance, there was a sign which read "PO HEADQUARTERS".

"Here we are," said Ms Wiz, jumping off her chair. "The headquarters of the Paranormal Operatives."

41

"I always thought PO stood for Post Office," said Carl.

"So do a lot of people," said Ms Wiz with a smile. "They keep sending their parcels here."

"That explains why the post is always late," Carl muttered as he followed Ms Wiz through some glass doors and into the building.

At first he thought that the office reception area was like any other. Then he noticed that all the people working there had black nail varnish. And that there was a sign on the wall which said "REMEMBER! WE ARE NOT WITCHES! WE ARE PARANORMAL OPERATIVES." And that a secretary nearby was reading a book called *Notions for Potions – Some Paranormal Recipes* while the keyboard beside her worked itself.

Ms Wiz walked up to the reception desk.

"I have urgent business with the travel department," she told the receptionist.

"Would that be time travel, space travel, inter-continental travel, inter-galactic travel, underwater travel, mind travel or holiday bookings?" the woman asked, filing one of her black fingernails.

"I need to get some children back from the other side of the world," said Ms Wiz.

"That'll be inter-continental travel," said the receptionist sleepily. "Mr Broom, our inter-continental travel executive, has gone for lunch in the Seychelles."

"Then get him back," said Ms Wiz sharply.

"I don't have the spell, do I?" said the woman.

"Who has got it?" asked Carl, thinking that at this rate they would never get Class Three back by the end of the day.

The woman looked at him coldly.

"Mr Broom," she said. "And he's gone for—"

"Enough!" Ms Wiz slammed the desk. "If you don't want to spend the rest of the day as a toad, you'll get him right now."

The woman shrugged. "Room 305 on the third floor," she said. "I'll see what I can do."

When Ms Wiz and Carl reached Room 305, they found a young man wearing a bathing suit and dark glasses sitting behind the desk.

"This had better be important," he said moodily. "I was just going for a swim in the sea when I was called back."

"It is," said Ms Wiz. "It's a case of missing children."

Mr Broom frowned as Ms Wiz explained the situation. Then he turned to a computer beside his desk and tapped some keys on the keyboard. Within seconds, a tropical scene appeared on the screen.

"There appears to be some sort of beach party going on," said Mr Broom. "Can you see any of your friends, young man?"

Carl moved nearer to the screen. "There's Podge at the barbecue," he said suddenly. "And Katrina's dancing by the radio. Mr Warlock seems to be asleep under a tree."

"Are you sure you want to get them back?" asked Mr Broom. "They seem to be having a very good time."

"Absolutely," said Ms Wiz. "All good things come to an end."

"Well, first of all you have to get the magic darts," said Mr Broom.

"But they're at St Barnabas," said Ms Wiz. "And I'm not allowed back."

Mr Broom shrugged. "Then you'll just have to find someone to work the spell for you," he said.

And suddenly Ms Wiz was smiling at Carl.

CHAPTER FIVE

Small Is Beautiful

There were times when Carl wished
that he wasn't late for everything,
and that afternoon, as he walked
through the gates of St Barnabas
carrying a pencil case, was one of
them. If it hadn't been for the cat
following him this morning, he would
be with Class Three now, enjoying
the sun and sand of Sombrero.

Instead he was the only person in
the world who could bring them back
and save Ms Wiz from getting into
more trouble. He was going to cast
a spell, like a real Paranormal
Operative. It was a bit dangerous, Ms
Wiz had said, but she trusted him.

As far as Carl could remember, this
was the first time that anyone had

ever trusted him with anything.

The School Inspector was pacing up and down inside the school gates like a watchdog.

"What are you doing, young man?" he asked suspiciously.

Carl held up the pencil case that Mr Broom at PO Headquarters had given him.

"I forgot my pencil case," he said. "I went home to fetch it."

The School Inspector did not look entirely convinced. "You haven't seen that Ms Wiz woman, have you?" he asked. "She seems to have vanished into thin air."

"That's because you banned her," said Carl.

"Hmm," said the School Inspector. "Just as long as she's not lurking about somewhere."

Inside the pencil case, Ms Wiz clung on to a fountain pen for dear life. She had agreed to help Carl with the travelling spell by making herself small enough to be smuggled into school.

From inside the case, she heard Carl telling the School Inspector that he had to fetch his books from Class Three's room so that he could work in the library. The pencil case shook as he ran across the playground.

Once again Ms Wiz gripped the fountain pen.

"The things I do for magic," she sighed.

As soon as they were in the classroom, Carl opened the case and carefully lifted Ms Wiz on to the desk.

"There's no time to lose," she said. "Grab the darts and I'll tell you the spell you've got to say."

"*I've* got to say?"

"I thought you wanted to see Sombrero," said Ms Wiz.

"I do, but—"

"Fine," smiled Ms Wiz. "You've got half an hour to travel across the world and bring your friends back. It's a piece of cake."

"What will you do while I'm away?" Carl asked.

"I suppose I'll have to hide in this case," said Ms Wiz. "The School

Inspector seems to be looking out for me."

"I won't be long," said Carl, holding the darts tightly in his hand. Repeating the words after Ms Wiz, he muttered the spell. Suddenly there was a humming noise and, for a few seconds, Carl felt like an arrow flying through the air, buffeted by the wind. He squeezed his eyes shut until the shaking stopped. Then he heard voices.

"Hey, it's Carl."

"What's he doing here?"

"Late as usual."

"Wake up, Carl. You're just in time for the limbo competition."

Slowly Carl opened his eyes. It was warm. The sunlight was dazzling. He could hear the distant sound of waves. And, all around him, were the children of Class Three.

"Phew," said Carl, dusting himself down. "I made it."

"Come and do the limbo," said Katrina. "You have to lean back and dance under this low pole. It's great."

Carl looked doubtful. "We haven't got much time before we have to get back," he said.

"Carl worrying about the time," Jack laughed. "I've heard everything now."

"All right," said Carl. "Someone go and wake up Mr Warlock. I'll have a

quick limbo and then we'll be on
our way."

Back at St Barnabas, Ms Wiz sat in the
darkness of Mr Broom's pencil case
and thought about the past.
  She remembered her adventures
with the children of Class Three – the
prizegiving when Mr Gilbert was
turned into a sheep, the time when a

local hospital was invaded by white mice, the hunt for Lizzie's stolen cat, the day when Jack let loose ghosts and demons in a library, her adventures in a television set with Caroline and Little Musha.

"I've certainly been there whenever magic was needed," she said to herself. "But maybe it's time to move to another school. Or even to another country."

She paced up and down in the darkness. Carl had been gone almost ten minutes now. What if the spell had sent him to the wrong place? Or he couldn't remember how to get back? Or he had lost the magic darts? If something happened to her friends, she would never forgive herself.

But then Ms Wiz smiled. Outside the pencil case, she heard a distant hum which grew louder and louder. Suddenly the classroom was alive with the sound of children's voices.

"Wow," Podge was saying. "I've just had the weirdest dream. I thought I was on a tropical island."

"That was no dream," Carl said. Ms Wiz felt the pencil case being lifted, its top opened slowly. She looked up and saw familiar faces looking down at her. "That was Wizardry," Carl smiled.

Ms Wiz climbed out of the pencil case and stood on the desk. It was difficult behaving like a serious Head Teacher when you were only three inches tall, but she had to give it a try.

"Now where's Mr Warlock?" she asked.

"He wanted to go straight home," said Carl. "So I gave him the spell and the second dart."

"I think he was embarrassed at being unable to get us back," said Lizzie.

"Quite right too," said Ms Wiz. "Now, since I've been banned from the school, Carl is going to have to smuggle me out."

"What happens if the School Inspector asks where we've been?" asked Jack.

Ms Wiz straightened her back and looked at him sternly. "You should say, 'I cannot tell a—'"

"I think we should lie," said Carl firmly. "Just this once."

"All right," said Ms Wiz. "Say you went to a museum."

At that moment, there was a loud thudding noise on the roof of the classroom.

"That will be Class Four," smiled Ms Wiz. "Miss N Chanter's very punctual. Can they get down all right?"

"There's a ladder leading down from the roof," said Katrina.

"Good," said Ms Wiz, as a pigeon appeared at the window, hovered for a moment and then flew off. "Miss Chanter's off home." She glanced at a clock on the wall. "It's time for you all to go too. Your parents will be waiting for you."

"When will we see you again?" asked Podge.

"Well, right now I'm going to take a holiday," said Ms Wiz, reaching inside the pencil case and pulling out some bright yellow trousers. "I've even brought my holiday clothes."

"But you'll be back, won't you?" asked Caroline. "Whenever magic's needed?"

Ms Wiz paused as she climbed back into the case. "I hope so," she said with a smile, before closing the lid over her head.

Carl walked home slowly. Just once he looked inside the case. There, in

the corner, was the tiny black dress of
a head teacher.

Carefully putting it into his jacket
pocket, Carl went over the strange,
magical events of the day, wondering
whether he would ever see his
paranormal friend again. He smiled
at the thought of her.

" 'Bye, Ms Wiz," he said quietly.

Books in this series available from Macmillan

The prices shown below are correct at the time of going to press. However, Macmillan Publishers reserve the right to show new retail prices on covers which may differ from those previously advertised.

All Macmillan titles can be ordered at your local bookshop or are available by post from:

**Book Service by Post
PO Box 29, Douglas, Isle of Man IM99 1BQ**

Credit cards accepted. For details:
Telephone: 01624 675137
Fax: 01624 670923
E-mail: bookshop@enterprise.net

Free postage and packing in the UK.
Overseas customers: add £1 per book (paperback)
and £3 per book (hardback)